THE TALE OF

MRS TIGGY-WINKLE

BEATRIX POTTER

KALEIDOSCOPE BOOKS

O nce upon a time there was a little girl called Lucie, who lived at a farm called Littletown. She was a good little girl — only she was always losing her pocket-handkerchiefs!

One day little Lucie came into the farm-yard crying — oh, she did cry so! 'I've lost my pocket-handkin! Three handkins and a pinny! Have *you* seen them, Tabby Kitten?'

The Kitten went on washing her white paws; so Lucie asked a speckled hen —

'Sally Henny-penny, have *you* found three pocket-handkins?'

But the speckled hen ran into a barn, clucking —

'I go barefoot, barefoot, bare-foot!'

And then Lucie asked Cock Robin sitting on a twig.

Cock Robin looked sideways at Lucie with his bright black eye, and he flew over a stile and away.

Lucie climbed upon the stile and looked up at the hill behind Little-town — a hill that goes up — up — into the clouds as though it had no top!

And a great way up the hillside she thought she saw some white things spread upon the grass.

Lucie scrambled up the hill as fast as her stout legs would carry her; she ran along a steep path-way — up and up — until Little-town was right away down below — she could have dropped a pebble down the chimney!

Presently she came to a spring, bubbling out from the hill-side.

Some one had stood a tin can upon a stone to catch the water — but the water was already running over, for the can was no bigger than an egg-cup! And where the sand upon the path was wet — there were footmarks of a *very* small person.

Lucie ran on, and on.

The path ended under a big rock. The grass was short and green, and there were clothes-props cut from bracken stems, with lines of plaited rushes, and a heap of tiny clothes pins — but no pocket-handkerchiefs!

But there was something else — a door! straight into the hill; and inside it some one was singing —

'Lily-white and clean, oh!
With little frills between, oh!
 Smooth and hot — red rusty spot
Never here be seen, oh!'

Lucie, knocked — once — twice, and interrupted the song. A little frightened voice called out 'Who's that?'

Lucie opened the door: and what do you think there was inside the hill? — a nice clean kitchen with a flagged floor and wooden beams — just like any other farm kitchen. Only the ceiling was so low that Lucie's head nearly touched it; and the pots and pans were small, and so was everything there.

There was a nice hot singey smell; and at the table, with an iron in her hand stood a very stout short person staring anxiously at Lucie.

Her print gown was tucked up, and she was wearing a large apron over her striped petticoat. Her little black nose went sniffle, sniffle, snuffle, and her eyes went twinkle, twinkle; and underneath her cap — where Lucie had yellow curls — that little person had PRICKLES!

'Who are you?' said Lucie. 'Have you seen my pocket-handkins?'

The little person made a bob-curtsey — 'Oh, yes, if you please'm; my name is Mrs Tiggy-winkle; oh, yes if you please'm, I'm an excellent clear-starcher!' And she took something out of a clothes-basket, and spread it on the ironing-blanket.

'What's that thing?' said Lucie — 'that's not my pocket-hand-kin?'

'Oh no, if you pleas'm; that's a little scarlet waist-coat belonging to Cock Robin!'

And she ironed it and folded it, and put it on one side.

Then she took something else off a clothes-horse —

'That isn't my pinny?' said Lucie.

'Oh no, if you pleas'm; that's a damask table-cloth belonging to Jenny Wren; look how it's stained with currant wine!' said Mrs Tiggy-winkle.

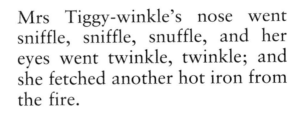

Mrs Tiggy-winkle's nose went sniffle, sniffle, snuffle, and her eyes went twinkle, twinkle; and she fetched another hot iron from the fire.

'There's one of my pocket-handkins!' cried Lucie — 'and there's my pinny!'

Mrs Tiggy-winkle ironed it, and goffered it, and shook out the frills.

'Oh that *is* lovely!' said Lucie.

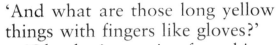

'And what are those long yellow things with fingers like gloves?'

'Oh, that's a pair of stockings belonging to Sally Henny-penny — look how she's worn the heels out with scratching in the yard! She'll very soon go barefoot!' said Mrs Tiggy-winkle.

'Why, there's another handker-
sniff — but it isn't mine; it's red?'

'Oh no, if you please'm; that
one belongs to old Mrs Rabbit;
and it *did* so smell of onions! I've
had to wash it separately, I can't
get out the smell.'

'There's another one of mine,'
said Lucie.

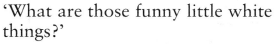

'What are those funny little white things?'

'That's a pair of mittens belonging to Tabby Kitten; I only have to iron them; she washes them herself.'

'There's my last pocket-handkin!' said Lucie.

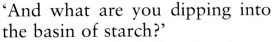

'And what are you dipping into the basin of starch?'

'They're little dicky shirt-fronts belonging to Tom Titmouse — most terrible particular!' said Mrs Tiggy-winkle. 'Now I've finished my ironing; I'm going to air some clothes.'

'What are these dear soft fluffy things?' said Lucie.

'Oh those are woolly coats belonging to the little lambs at Skelghyl.'

'Will their jackets take off?' asked Lucie.

'Oh yes, if you please'm; look at the sheep-mark on the shoulder. And here's one marked for Gates-garth, and three that come from Little-town. They're *always* marked at washing!' said Mrs Tiggy-winkle.

And she hung up all sorts and sizes of clothes — small brown coats of mice; and one velvety black moleskin waist-coat; and a red tail-coat with no tail belonging to Squirrel Nutkin; and a very much shrunk blue jacket belonging to Peter Rabbit; and a petticoat, not marked, that had gone lost in the washing — and at last the basket was empty!

Then Mrs Tiggy-winkle made tea
— a cup for herself and a cup for
Lucie. They sat before the fire on
a bench and looked sideways at
one another. Mrs Tiggy-winkle's
hand, holding the tea-cup, was
very very brown, and very very
wrinkly with the soap-suds; and
all through her gown and her cap,
there were *hairpins* sticking
wrong end out; so that Lucie
didn't like to sit too near her.

When they had finished tea, they tied up the clothes in bundles; and Lucie's pocket-handkerchiefs were folded up inside her clean pinny, and fastened with a silver safety-pin.

And then they made up the fire with turf, and came out and locked the door, and hid the key under the door-sill.

Then away down the hill trotted Lucie and Mrs Tiggy-winkle with the bundles of clothes!

All the way down the path little animals came out of the fern to meet them; the very first that they met were Peter Rabbit and Benjamin Bunny!

And she gave them their nice clean clothes; and all the little animals and birds were so very much obliged to dear Mrs Tiggy-winkle.

So that at the bottom of the hill when they came to the stile, there was nothing left to carry except Lucie's one little bundle.

Lucie scrambled up the stile with the bundle in her hand; and then she turned to say 'Good-night,' and to thank the washer-woman — But what a *very* odd thing! Mrs Tiggy-winkle had not waited either for thanks or for the washing bill!

She was running running running up the hill — and where was her white frilled cap? and her shawl? and her gown — and her petticoat?

And *how* small she had grown
— and *how* brown — and cov-
ered with PRICKLES!

Why! Mrs Tiggy-winkle was
nothing but a HEDGEHOG.

(Now some people say that little Lucie had been asleep upon the
stile — but then how could she
have found three clean pocket-
handkins and a pinny, pinned
with a silver safety-pin?

And beside — *I* have seen that
door into the back of the hill
called Cat Bells — and besides *I*
am very well acquainted with
dear Mrs Tiggy-winkle!)

THE END

This edition published exclusively for
Kaleidoscope Books in 1986 by
Octopus Books Inc
1 Madison Avenue
New York NY 10010

Kaleidoscope Books is the exclusive imprint
of B. Dalton Booksellers, Minneapolis,
Minnesota

This edition © 1986 Octopus Books Inc
ISBN: 0 8300 0440 8
Printed in the United States of America